DO YOU HAVE A TALKING HAT?

by Cindy Cage

Housetop Publishing
Greensboro, NC

Housetop Publishing
Greensboro, NC 27410
www.housetoppublishing.com

Copyright © 2024 Cindy Cage

All rights reserved. No part of this book may be reproduced or transmitted in any form or by any means, electronic or mechanical, including photocopying, recording, or by any information storage or retrieval system, without written permission from the publisher.

For information address:
Email: cindycage@me.com
or www.cindycage.com

The text in this book is hand drawn.
The illustrations are digitally drawn.

ISBN 978-1-951224-17-2

Manufactured in United States
2 4 6 8 10 9 7 5 3 1

A Special Thanks to Benjamin Masaki Adachi:

I read my grandson this manuscript and asked him to sketch the kind of hats the descriptions represented to him. My illustrations were based off his creative ideas.

Ben is the author and illustrator of *That Is Ridiculous,*
Housetop Publishing, Greensboro, NC.

If the hat you wear could talk,

it could tell me about you.

"You are going somewhere fancy."

"You are sitting in the sunshine."

"You love driving really fast."

"You are someone from the future."

"You're an educated person."

"You're a king with lots of gold."

"You are standing in the cold."

"You're the leader of a band."

"You're the driver of a train."

"You are called to put out fires."

"You are piloting a plane."

"You love cooking fine French food."

"You enjoy when it is raining."

Hats are made to cover heads,

but they do much more than that.

Do you have a talking hat?

hard hat	pilgrim hat
derby hat	pith helmet
sun hat	auto racing helmet

futuristic hat

top hat

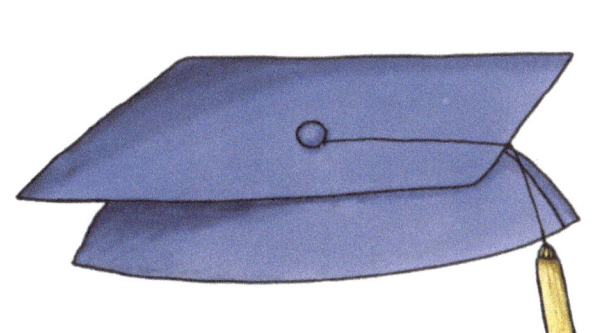
morterboard

royal diadem

party hat

beanie

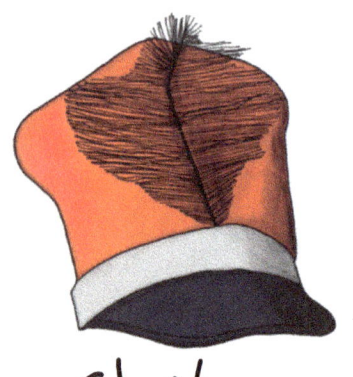
shako

hog head hat

firefighter helmet

peaked cap

Santa hat

chef's toque

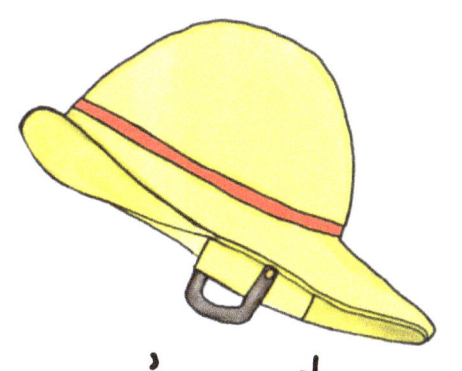
sou'wester

jester hat

pirate hat

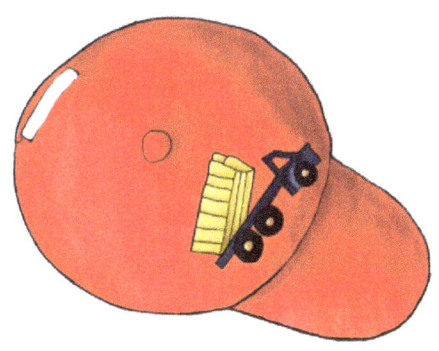
baseball cap

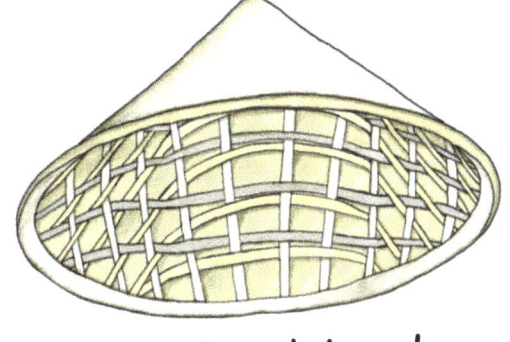
conical hat

cartwheel hat

www.ingramcontent.com/pod-product-compliance
Lightning Source LLC
Chambersburg PA
CBHW040013080526
44586CB00028B/2988